Secret Kingdom

Special thanks to Linda Chapman

To Sarah Hawkins, for making the
Secret Kingdom the magical,
wonderful place it is!

ORCHARD BOOKS
338 Euston Road, London NW1 3BH
Orchard Books Australia
Level 17/207 Kent Street, Sydney, NSW 2000
A Paperback Original

First published in 2012 by Orchard Books

Text © Hothouse Fiction Limited 2012

Illustrations © Orchard Books 2012

A CIP catalogue record for this book is available
from the British Library.

ISBN 978 1 40832 369 4

10

Printed and bound by CPI Group (UK) Ltd, Croydon, CR0 4YY

The paper and board used in this paperback are natural recyclable
products made from wood grown in sustainable forests. The
manufacturing processes conform to the environmental regulations
of the country of origin.

Orchard Books is a division of Hachette Children's Books,
an Hachette UK company

www.hachette.co.uk

Series created by Hothouse Fiction

www.hothousefiction.com

Glitter Beach

ROSIE BANKS

ORCHARD

Contents

The Adventure Begins

"Hi, Mum! I'm home!"

Ellie Macdonald ran into the empty kitchen through the back door. She shrugged her schoolbag off her shoulders and put it down carefully. After all, there was something very special inside! At the bottom, wrapped up in her school jumper, was a mysterious wooden box.

As she opened her bag, Ellie felt a flicker of excitement. She and her best friends, Summer and Jasmine, were the only ones who knew that the box was much more than an ordinary jewellery box. It had been made by the ruler of a magical land called the Secret Kingdom, where incredible creatures like fairies, mermaids, unicorns and pixies lived. It was a wonderful place, but it was in terrible trouble.

When everyone in the land had decided they wanted kind King Merry to rule rather than his horrid sister, Queen Malice, the evil queen had sent six thunderbolts crashing into different parts of the kingdom. Each thunderbolt had the power to make trouble and bring great unhappiness. Ellie and her friends

had promised to help stop the nasty
queen. Whenever one of her thunderbolts
caused a problem in the Secret Kingdom,
a riddle would appear in the lid of the
Magic Box to tell the girls where they
were needed. When they had solved it,
Ellie, Summer and Jasmine would be
whisked away to the kingdom to try
and help. They had already had five
wonderful adventures and Ellie couldn't
wait for the magic to work again!

Ellie pulled the Magic Box out of her
bag and looked hopefully at the carvings
of amazing creatures that covered
every side, and the glittering jewels that
decorated its mirrored lid. If only the lid
would start glowing, that would mean it
was time for her and her friends to return
to the Secret Kingdom. But all she could

see was her own reflection, her red curls falling messily around her face.

Ellie sighed and carried the box to the

hall carefully. She caught sight of her mum through the window, tidying up the hanging baskets in the front garden. Ellie avoided her and headed for the stairs, clutching the Magic Box.

"RARRRRR!" With a loud yell, Molly, Ellie's little sister, jumped out from where she had been hiding beside the hall table.

Ellie almost dropped the box in shock. "Molly!"

Molly whooped in delight. "I made you jump, Ellie!" She was four and looked just like Ellie had when she was little, with red curls that reached to her shoulders and mischievous green eyes. She loved to play tricks on her big sister. "What's that?" she said curiously, spotting the box in Ellie's arms.

"Nothing."

"Let me see!" Molly tried to look.

"It's just an old box, Mol," Ellie told her hastily. The last thing she wanted was Molly looking in the Magic Box! Inside

it were six wooden compartments, and
five of them were filled with the special
objects Ellie and the others had collected
on their adventures. There was a magic
moving map of the Secret Kingdom,
a tiny silver unicorn horn that let the
person holding it talk to animals, a cloud
crystal that could be used to control
the weather, a pearl that could turn
you invisible and an icy hourglass that
could be used to freeze time. If Molly
found those things she'd want to know
where they had come from and the girls
couldn't tell anyone about the Secret
Kingdom!

Ellie swooped the box over her sister's
head and put it on the table. Then,
jumping forward, she started to tickle
Molly to distract her.

Molly squealed and pushed her away. "Ellie, get off!"

Ellie tickled her harder. "Nope! I'm the tickle monster and I'm coming to get you!" she teased, chasing her around the hall.

Molly laughed and shrieked. "Get off me! Get off… *hic!*" A loud hiccup exploded from her and both sisters burst out laughing.

The front door opened. Mrs Macdonald
looked in. "What's going on, girls?"

Molly could barely contain her giggles.
"Ellie was tickling me, Mummy, and now
I've got… I've got… *Hic!*"

"Hiccups," Ellie finished for her with a
grin.

"Oh, Molly." Mrs Macdonald shook her
head. "Come on, let's get you some water.
Did you have a good day at school,
Ellie?" she called over her shoulder as she
led Molly away.

"Yes, fine, thanks, Mum. I'm just going
up to my room for a while."

Grabbing the Magic Box, Ellie ran
upstairs. After putting the box safely on
her desk and changing out of her school
clothes, she got out her sketchbook and
began to draw a picture of Trixi, the little

royal pixie who the girls had met on all
their adventures. Ellie was very good at
art, but she still couldn't make the pixie
look as cheeky and friendly as she was in
real life.

Taking a rest for the moment, she
glanced up at the box and almost fell off
her chair in surprise.

It was glowing.

Ellie gasped and jumped to her feet,
sending her pencil
pot flying. "Oh
wow! It's time
for another
adventure!"

She threw
her school
jumper over
the box in case

anyone happened to come in and see it,
and ran downstairs to use the phone. She
had to tell Jasmine and Summer straight
away!

"Promise you won't look at the riddle
on the box until we get there!" begged
Jasmine when Ellie called her.

"I won't!" Ellie promised, although
she was desperate to find out what the
riddle would say, and where in the Secret
Kingdom they were needed this time.

Ellie waited impatiently by the front
door. Jasmine and Summer both lived in
Honeyvale Village too, but it seemed to
take them ages to arrive. Each minute
felt like an hour! At last, she saw Summer
running along the street, her blonde
pigtails flying out behind her. At the same
time Jasmine came racing around the

corner on her bike.

"It's really happening then?" Jasmine breathed, pulling off her bike helmet, her dark hair tumbling around her shoulders.

"Yes!" Ellie said, happiness fizzing through her.

They hurried inside. "Hi, girls," Mrs Macdonald called from the kitchen. "Are you staying for tea?"

"Yes, please," Summer and Jasmine both chorused.

"Though hopefully we'll have had an amazing adventure before then!" Jasmine whispered to Ellie and Summer. The girls knew that time in the real world stayed still when they were in the Secret Kingdom, so Ellie's mum would never even notice that they'd been gone. They shared a smile and raced upstairs.

"Ta-da!" Ellie whisked her jumper off the box.

"Look!" Summer squealed. "We're really going to the Secret Kingdom again!"

"Who do you think we'll meet this time?" said Jasmine.

"Let's see what the riddle says!" Ellie carefully read out the words that had formed in the mirror:

"Danger from a royal hand,
A thunderbolt in sparkling sand,
A wicked deed must be put right,
Before the next midsummer night."

The girls looked at one another in confusion. "What does that mean?" said Summer, twiddling the end of one of her plaits. "Where do we have to go?"

Suddenly the box opened and a piece
of parchment floated out of it. It was the
magic map!

Ellie carefully unfolded it, with
Summer and Jasmine peering over her
shoulders. The map glowed with colour.
Magical pictures on it showed what was
happening on the crescent-shaped island
of the Secret Kingdom, with its emerald
green hills and meadows, aquamarine
waters and sandy coves.

"Look! There's Unicorn Valley!" said
Summer, looking down to where unicorns
were cantering far below, their silver and
gold horns glittering in the sunshine.

"And Magic Mountain," said Jasmine,
pointing to a huge snow-covered
mountain which had pixies all over it,
skiing and zooming down enormous
slides made of ice.

"I wonder where we're needed this

time?" said Ellie, her forehead crinkling in thought as she looked at the riddle again.

"It says 'a thunderbolt in sparkling sand'," said Summer. "Well, you get sand at the seaside – so maybe we have to go to a beach?"

"Glitter Beach!" gasped Jasmine, pointing to a label next to a little harbour with shops and boats. "Somewhere with a name like that is bound to have sparkling sand."

Ellie and Summer nodded eagerly.

Jasmine's hazel eyes shone in excitement. "What are we waiting for? Let's call Trixi!"

The girls put their hands on the green gems of the box and looked at one another. "The answer to the riddle is Glitter Beach!" they said together.

A Fairy Festival

There was a flash of light, and the
drawings on Ellie's bedroom walls
fluttered. The light was so bright that
Ellie, Jasmine and Summer all blinked. As
their eyes flew open they heard a tinkling
laugh. A familiar little pixie was hovering
in front of them on a floating leaf!

"Trixibelle!" cried Jasmine happily.
"You've come to take us on another
adventure!"

"Hello, girls. It's lovely to see you again!" Trixi smiled.

"You look pretty!" Ellie said, looking at her pixie friend, who was wearing a bright yellow dress made out of sunflower petals and a pair of pretty sunglasses. A garland of multicoloured flowers hung around her neck.

"I was just getting ready to go on holiday!" Trixi flew a loop-the-loop on her leaf. "I'm so excited about it! My fairy friend, Willow, has invited me to

go to a special ceremony with her. All
the fairies in the kingdom meet up every
Midsummer's Eve to watch the kingdom's
magic being renewed – and I'm going
too!"

Her words reminded Ellie of the Magic
Box. "Oh!" she exclaimed. "The riddle
said something about midsummer."

Trixi stopped twirling. "Goodness! I
was so excited about my holiday I forgot
that I normally only see you when
something's gone wrong! Where did the
Magic Box say the next thunderbolt is?"

"A place with sparkling sand," Ellie
told her. "We think that might mean
Glitter Beach."

Trixi read the riddle in the mirror
on the Magic Box, and her blue eyes
widened. "But that's where all the fairies

are going! Oh no! Perhaps Queen
Malice's horrible thunderbolt is going to
ruin the fairy holiday!"

"Don't worry," Ellie said quickly, seeing
the pixie's alarmed expression. "We'll
come with you to Glitter Beach. If a
thunderbolt has landed there, we'll soon
fix things!"

"Oh, thank you!" Trixi said gratefully.
She tapped her magic ring and chanted:

*"The evil queen has trouble planned.
Brave helpers fly to save our land!"*

As she spoke, the thunderbolt
riddle faded and her words formed
in the mirror. Ellie's purple bedroom
walls disappeared and the girls were
surrounded by shards of sunlight. Jasmine,

Ellie and Summer grabbed one another's hands just in time as the magic whirled them away!

Round and round they turned until the magic set them down gently. There was the feel of sunshine on their skin and a gentle rocking under their feet.

"Wow!" Ellie breathed as she opened her eyes. They were standing in a boat made out of a large white shell, which was being pulled by two huge silver dolphins. The aquamarine water splashed over their backs as they plunged through the waves, leaving a trail of snowy foam behind them. The sun shone down brightly from the forget-me-not-blue sky as they headed towards a small harbour with a shimmering beach.

"We're tiny!" Ellie realised suddenly as she saw that she was the same height as Trixi.

The others both gasped.

'That's why the dolphins look so big!" said Summer.

"I thought I had better make you small or you wouldn't be able to enjoy Glitter Beach properly. There's lots to see and do but it's all built for fairies!" Trixi explained.

"It's just amazing being this small," said Summer, throwing her arms around Trixi.

"It's lovely to be able to hug you!"

Ellie put her hand to the top of her head to check for the tiara that always appeared when she went to the Secret Kingdom, to show that she was an important friend and helper of King Merry. Sure enough, it was there, reduced to teeny-tiny size just as Ellie was. Jasmine and Summer were wearing theirs too.

"Glitter Beach is just ahead." Trixi waved an arm towards the harbour. The girls could just see pretty little shops and market stalls in the bay, and multicoloured boats tied to the pier.

"Look, the boats have got wings instead of sails!" Jasmine called out as they got closer.

Trixi managed to smile. "That's because

those are fairy yachts. They fly as well as sail in the water!"

"And look at the surfers!" exclaimed Ellie.

All around them, fairies were surfing on long, flat, mussel shells. Dressed in colourful bikinis or swimming trunks, they raced across the waves, some balancing with their arms out, others spinning around or flying up into the air before landing back on their boards, their wings shimmering in the sunlight.

One was even doing a handstand on his board, keeping his balance by moving his wings delicately. He came zooming past the girls, sending a wave splashing all over them.

They squealed. "Sorry!" he called.

"We don't mind!" called Ellie, splashing him back.

"Oh, this is amazing!" said Jasmine, pushing back her long dark hair.

"This is one of my favourite places in the whole kingdom," Trixi said. "And it's so important. At twelve o'clock every Midsummer's Eve the golden sand turns to glitter dust for one minute. In that time all the magic is returned to the land for another year. The fairies always come to watch it happen, but I've never seen it before – I can't wait!" Trixi looked down at her pixie ring. "I've had to do so many spells for King Merry this year that my magic's nearly all used up! Without the sand at Glitter Beach there would be no magic anywhere in the Secret Kingdom."

"Oh, wow!" breathed Ellie. "Can we watch it happen?"

"Of course," replied Trixi.

Summer had a thought. "Will… will the glitter dust give us magic, too?"

Trixi's forehead wrinkled. "I don't know. But tonight is an extra-magical night. Anything could happen!"

"Even if we could only do magic for a little while, it would be brilliant!" said Jasmine, giving the others an excited look.

"We can't forget about Queen Malice's thunderbolt though," Summer warned. "Remember, we have to find it before it causes trouble."

Ellie and Jasmine nodded. They really did have to watch out! There was no telling what horrible things Queen Malice might have planned.

The dolphins pulled up to the wooden pier and the girls climbed out of the shell boat. Pushing their heads out of the water, the dolphins opened their mouths in toothy grins. Summer reached up on tiptoe and patted one on the nose. "Thank you for the lift!" she cried happily.

The dolphins made a clicking noise that sounded like *"you're welcome!"*

As Trixi flew her leaf out of the boat another fairy rushed over and hugged her. She was wearing a bright blue dress with a red flower at the shoulder. Her delicate wings were as aquamarine as the sea, and she had wild flowers in her hair.

"Hello!" she said delightedly.

"Ellie, Summer and Jasmine, this is my fairy friend, Willow," Trixi introduced them.

Willow stared at their tiaras. "You must be the human girls who've been finding Queen Malice's thunderbolts and solving all the problems they cause!" she exclaimed, her wings fluttering.

Ellie nodded.

Willow grinned. "I'm so glad to meet you. We're all so grateful to you for all your help fighting Queen Malice."

Trixi shook her head sadly. "We think that she's sent a thunderbolt here to Glitter Beach."

"Oh no!" Willow gasped.

"We have to find it before it ruins the ceremony," Ellie added. "Will you help us look?"

"Of course," Willow replied, her wings fluttering anxiously. "I'll ask at the harbour and see if anyone's noticed it."

"We'll check the town," Trixi said.

Willow flew off towards the sea, and the girls and Trixi carried on towards the shops.

"I wish we could be here without

the thunderbolt threatening to ruin everything." Ellie sighed, looking around at the market stalls piled high with beautiful things, and the old-fashioned shops with baskets of bright flowers hanging outside. "I'd love to come to Glitter Beach on holiday!"

Summer and Jasmine agreed. "It is such a pretty place," Summer said. "That's why we can't let Queen Malice wreck it!"

"Let's split up," Jasmine suggested. "We can meet at the clock tower when it strikes eight," she said, pointing at the shimmering silver clock tower in the centre of the town square.

"Shout if you spot anything!" Ellie called as she rushed into the nearest shop.

Summer looked around the stalls, where there were fairies selling tiny polished

rings made out of wood and bracelets
and clothes stitched from leaves, some
green and spring-like and some in the
beautiful golden and red colours of
autumn.

She talked to a pretty fairy who was
selling gorgeous shell boxes and necklaces
as well as delicate golden sand castles.
But she hadn't seen anything suspicious.

Jasmine walked over to a stall heaped with delicious-looking treats and read the labels. "Icicle snaps, honeydew drops, rose candyfloss." They all looked so yummy that her tummy rumbled loudly! But there was no time to stop and taste them – she had a thunderbolt to find!

As the sound of eight bells rang out across the sea, Trixi and the girls rushed over to the clock tower, shaking their heads as they saw one another.

"There's no sign of trouble anywhere," Trixi sighed.

"There's nothing at the harbour, either," Willow said as she landed next to them.

But just then Ellie caught sight of something in the sky. "What's that?" she asked. The others followed her gaze. A dark cloud seemed to be heading across the water towards Glitter Beach.

"It looks like a tornado!" exclaimed
Jasmine.

The cloud coming towards the beach
was shaped like a funnel and was swirling
round and round. There were cries of
alarm as the fairies
noticed it too.

"Quick! It's a
whirlwind! Get
inside!" The
shouts rang out.

Trixibelle
jumped on her leaf
and zoomed
over to
the girls.
"Follow me!"
she called,

hurrying them inside a shop behind lots of worried fairies. They crouched beside a display of tiny acorn cups and peeked through the window, looking out to the beach where the tornado was whirling closer, sweeping up boats and abandoned mussel-shell surfboards in its path.

"Look!" Summer cried as the whirlwind reached the beach and all the beautiful golden sand started to swirl up from the ground into it. "It's taking all the sand!"

The fairies shouted, trying to cast spells to stop it – but nothing worked.

Just then Jasmine caught sight of figures moving in the swirling smoke. "Storm Sprites!" she cried, pointing at the shadowy shapes.

Summer and Ellie gasped as they

recognised the nasty creatures that were crouched on clouds moving round and round inside the whirling wind. The sprites screeched with laughter as the tornado whipped around faster and faster. Soon all the sand was gone, and the girls could see that the wind was coming from a jagged black shape in the rocky ground.

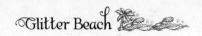

"It's the thunderbolt!" Summer breathed. It was buried deep in the earth, with just its black tip showing.

"It must have been under the sand!" Ellie gasped.

The sprites jeered and laughed as the tornado swept away.

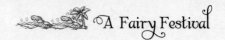

Everyone stared in disbelief. Every single grain of beautiful, sparkling sand had disappeared!

Queen Malice's Mischief

All that was left of the beach was dull rock. Ellie, Jasmine and Summer ran outside. Trixi and Willow stood next to them, close to tears. "This is awful!" Trixi cried. "What are we going to do? It's getting dark now, and if the sand's not here when the clock strikes twelve, no one in the kingdom will be able to do any magic for a whole year!"

"Don't worry," Ellie said, putting her arm around Trixi. "We'll break the thunderbolt and get the sand back before midnight."

Jasmine nodded. "We've defeated Queen Malice before and we can do it again!"

"There's no way we'll let her get away with this!" Summer vowed.

Trixi looked a little bit happier. "I'd better ask King Merry to come. He'll need to know what his rotten sister has been up to." Trixi tapped her ring and King Merry's name appeared in silvery letters in the air.

She tapped her ring a second time and, with a faint popping sound, the words vanished.

"I wonder how long it will take King Merry to arrive," Summer said.

"He'll come as soon as he gets the message," answered Trixi. "He's at the Enchanted Palace at the moment, so he can use the rainbow slide in the garden pond to get anywhere in the kingdom he wants."

"In the meantime we'd better start thinking of how we can sort this out!" said Jasmine determinedly.

The girls walked around the grey rocky beach, comforting all the fairies they met. Some were crying, others were staring around in horror or pointing at the thunderbolt. The girls hated seeing them so upset.

Suddenly, a few of the fairies started to point out to sea. The girls followed their gaze. There was a multicoloured glimmer in the air over the waves and where the rainbow met the water a rather stout person suddenly appeared.

"It's King Merry – and he's on water-skis!" gasped Jasmine.

The little round king headed towards them, a water-ski on each foot. He was holding on to green seaweed reins and two dolphins were towing him through the waves. He was wearing long, brightly patterned shorts and yellow armbands, as well as his half-moon spectacles. His cloak was blowing in the breeze and his crown was perched on top of a white sun hat.

"Hello, hello!" he cried as they ran to the edge of the water. Letting go of the reins with one hand, he tried to wave and lost his balance. His arms windmilled wildly. "Whoa!" he shouted in alarm.

"Oh dear!" Trixi's hand flew to her mouth as the king toppled backwards into the water. He bobbed around, held up by his armbands, while the dolphins circled around him in surprise. "Back in a minute!" Trixi cried as she zoomed over to him on her leaf.

Across the waves the girls saw her
tapping her pixie ring. The king rose
from the water and hovered above it, the
little pixie hovering around his shoulders.
She pointed to the shore and he began
to drift magically across the top of the
waves.

"Ah, very good, very good," the girls
heard him saying. "Excellent work, Trixi.
Hello, girls!" He waved to them again,
this time without falling over. Trixi's
magic put him gently down on the
beach, and Ellie, Summer and Jasmine
rushed over to him. Jasmine was normally
the same height as King Merry, but now
he loomed over her like a giant! The girls
suddenly felt very small. Trixi must have
noticed because she tapped her ring and
chanted:

"Back to human size you go,
Jasmine, Summer, Ellie – grow!"

The girls shot upwards until they were
back to normal. Ellie giggled to herself
as she realised that King Merry had

sunglasses on as well as his usual half-moon spectacles.

"I came as fast as I could," said the king anxiously. "What has my dreadful sister done now?"

"Her thunderbolt has stolen all the sand from Glitter Beach," Trixi cried. "There's not a single grain left, Your Majesty!"

"Oh, dearie me," King Merry sighed. He looked at the girls. "Have you got a plan to fix it?"

"Not yet," said Jasmine. "The tornado came and whisked the sand away so fast."

"Yes," Ellie added thoughtfully. "But where did it go after that? *Where* did the tornado take the sand?"

"I don't know," said Trixi. "I was too busy looking at the thunderbolt."

"Me too," said Summer.

"Maybe one of the fairies noticed," said Jasmine. "Let's ask around."

"Excellent idea!" King Merry declared.

"Um, maybe first, I might just…" Trixi flew around him and tapped her ring. His armbands disappeared in a bright flash.

The king smiled at her and adjusted his crown. "Oh, yes. Thank you, Trixi!"

The fairies were all hovering over the beach, talking anxiously. As King Merry and the girls walked over, they flocked around, talking all at once.

"Oh, please help us!" a little purple-winged fairy cried.

Summer, Ellie and Jasmine started asking the fairies about the tornado, but no one had watched where it went.

"It's no good," said Summer, sitting

down at last on the rocky beach. The
cloud of fairies fluttered overhead. Ellie
and Jasmine sat down too, and then Ellie
noticed a familiar-looking fairy flitting
nearby. She looked closely, and realised it
was Willow. She looked so tiny now!

"Hello," Ellie smiled and put out her
hand. The little fairy
landed on it, light as a
feather on her palm.
Willow looked at
them with wide
eyes. "Are you
going to help
us get the sand
back?"

"Yes," Jasmine told
her. "Don't worry,
we'll sort it out."

"But we've got to find out where the tornado went first," said Ellie. "And no one seems to have seen what happened to it."

"I did!" Willow declared.

They all stared at her in amazement.

"I watched it swirl into that cave over there," she continued, pointing to where there were some steep grey cliffs jutting out into the bay. The girls could just see a cave at the base of the cliffs.

"Brilliant!" said Jasmine. "Well done, Willow!" The little fairy beamed proudly.

After saying goodbye to Willow, the girls hurried across the beach.

"Look!" Jasmine hissed as they got closer to the cave. She pointed ahead. Even though it was dark, they could just make out lots of little spiky footprints in the mud around its entrance.

"Shhh," whispered Ellie. "Listen!"

Coming from the cave they could hear high, cackling voices.

"It's the Storm Sprites!" A shiver ran down Ellie's spine as she thought about Queen Malice's spiky-haired servants.

"What are they doing?" Summer asked shakily.

Jasmine squared her shoulders and looked at them both. "There's only one way to find out. Come on!"

A Cunning Plan

Jasmine, Summer and Ellie tiptoed up to
the cave entrance. It was a very big cave,
even though they were human-sized now.
As they got closer they could hear the
Storm Sprites shouting at one another.

"Hurry up!" one of them yelled. "Once
Queen Malice has this sand no one will
be able to get in her way any more!"

Summer gasped. Jasmine crept forwards and peered into the dark cave, and Ellie and Summer followed. Inside was a mountain of glittering golden sand. Eight Storm Sprites were shovelling it into sacks and stacking them up. The girls retreated a little way away from the cave's entrance.

"Willow was right," hissed Ellie. "The sand *is* in the cave!"

"And the sprites are going to take it to Queen Malice!" said Jasmine. "We've got to stop them!"

They stared at one another, wondering how.

"Yoo hoo! Girls!" a voice called, making them jump. King Merry was waving as he climbed clumsily over the rocks. Trixi was hovering behind him, holding his cloak up in the air.

"Shhh!" Jasmine hissed, rushing over to where the king was.

"We've found the sand!" she whispered.
"But we've found the Storm Sprites too!"

Trixi and the king looked very worried
as the girls explained what they had
seen. "But if they send the sand to Queen
Malice, everyone will lose their magic!"
King Merry said.

"We need to find a way to get it back,"
said Jasmine.

Ellie frowned thoughtfully. "Maybe we
can sneak in and take the sacks?"

"But the Storm Sprites will see us,"
Jasmine pointed out.

"The pearl!" Summer exclaimed.
"Don't you remember?" she asked as
everyone stared at her. "The mermaids
gave us a pearl that we could use to turn
ourselves invisible!"

There was a bright silver flash and

Summer gasped as a heavy weight fell into her arms. "The Magic Box!"

Ellie and Jasmine glanced at each other in delight. The Magic Box had a wonderful habit of appearing just when it was really needed!

King Merry looked proud. "It really was a very clever invention, wasn't it?" he said to Trixi.

"Exceptionally clever, Your Majesty."
Trixi smiled as the lid of the box slowly
started to open. Tucked inside one of
the little wooden compartments lay a
glowing, shimmering silver pearl.

"We can use this to make ourselves
invisible and get into the cave," Summer
breathed, taking the pearl out of the
box. Almost immediately her fingers and
hands vanished and then suddenly she
disappeared completely!

"Summer? Where have you gone?"
cried Jasmine. Then she jumped as
Summer poked her gently in the ribs.

"I'm still here!" Summer's voice came
from behind them. "Here, hold my hand."

Jasmine felt Summer's hand touch hers.
She grabbed Ellie's fingers with her other
hand. Holding on to one another, all

three girls were completely invisible!

"Trixi, what about you?' Jasmine asked from thin air.

"Mermaid magic won't work on the king and me," the pixie said. "I'm afraid you're going to have to do this on your own, girls."

"No problem," Jasmine said bravely. "We'll get the sand back!"

"Hopefully," Summer added rather nervously.

"Of course we will!" Ellie declared.

"Good luck!" Trixi and the king called.

Holding hands, the girls set off to the cave entrance. It was very dark inside, but they could hear the sprites talking to one another and shovelling the sand into the sacks. As their eyes got used to the darkness the girls could see the sprites'

bat-like wings folded against their backs.
Ellie, Summer and Jasmine held their
breath as they tiptoed further into the
cave, creeping towards the sand.

Clunk!

Ellie tripped over a spare shovel lying
on the ground and it banged noisily
against the rocks. The sprites looked up.
The girls froze, squeezing one another's
hands tightly. A horrible thought crossed
Jasmine's mind – the pearl would only
keep them invisible for a short while.
What if its magic wore off before they
got the sand back?

"What was that noise?" asked one
sprite.

"I don't know," said another. They
looked around suspiciously.

The girls stayed as still as they could.

Summer was sure the sprites must be
able to hear her heart hammering in her
chest.

The sprites slowly got back to work.
Jasmine continued to lead the way to
the back of the cave but as she did so,
she felt a sneeze building in her nose. She
swallowed, trying to hold it in, but it was
no good... all of a
sudden it burst out!

"Ahh-chooo!"

All the sprites
jumped.

"Who's
there?" one of
them called.

The girls
hardly dared to
breathe.

"Maybe... maybe it's a ghost," said the smallest sprite.

"Don't be a nincompoop," another sprite told him. "There's no such thing as ghosts."

But Ellie saw that all the sprites had started to look slightly worried. *That's it!* she thought, remembering how she had jumped when Molly had leapt out at her back at home. She tugged on Jasmine's hand and whispered as quietly as she could.

"If we pretend to be ghosts we'll scare them so much that they'll run away and we won't have to be invisible! There will be no chance of them coming back again, because they'll be too scared!"

Jasmine passed the message on to Summer and then kicked over a nearby sack.

The sprites jumped back in alarm as it fell.

"How did that happen?" one demanded.

"Ghosts!" said the smallest sprite, looking around in alarm. "I told you – it's ghosts!"

Jasmine took a deep breath and started to make a strange howling, moaning noise.

"Argh!" the sprites all yelled. The smallest sprite backed up so quickly he tripped over his spade and fell to the ground, sending the sprite next to him sprawling. The rest of the sprites started to scramble around as Ellie and then Summer joined in with ghostly noises. Jasmine kicked over two more bags. She was very good at acting and she put on her best spooky voice. "We're the ghosts of the Glitter Caves and we're coming to get youuuuuuuuuuu!"

The sprites started to yell and run around. As one ran near them, Ellie had an idea. Using her free hand, she reached out and tickled the sprite.

"Argh! Eee! Argh!" he yelled. "The ghost's got me!"

Ellie had to fight back her giggles.
"I am the Tickle Monster Ghost!" she
said in a spooky voice like Jasmine,
remembering how she had made Molly
squeal. "Beware! Bewaaaaaaaaaaare!" She
pulled the others around the cave, poking
and prodding at the sprites while Jasmine
made spooky noises and Summer pushed
the sacks over.

"Forget the silly magic sand!" the
smallest sprite shouted. "I'm getting out
of here!"

"Me too!" yelled another.

"Me three!" yelped the one on the floor.

All eight sprites charged to the entrance
of the cave, pushing and shoving one
another as they fled.

"We did it!" Summer said.

"And only just in time!" said Jasmine

as they all slowly shimmered into view again. The sprites ran off onto the rocky beach and charged straight down into the aquamarine sea. They flapped over the water, splashing and yelling about ghosts.

Ellie grinned. "That was fun!"

"And now we can get the sand back to

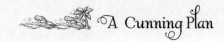

the beach!" said Jasmine.

"Noooooo!" A screech of rage rang through the cave. The girls jumped and swung around. Summer squeaked in alarm and the others caught their breath. There, standing right in the entrance of the cave, was Queen Malice herself!

Stolen Sand

The wicked queen's midnight-dark eyes flashed with fury.

She pointed at the girls with a bony finger. "I have had enough of your meddling, you interfering humans! How dare you keep coming to this land to stop my magic? You will not break my sixth thunderbolt!"

"Malice!" King Merry's voice rang out as he hurried to the cave entrance. "My dear, please stop behaving like this."

"Who are *you* to tell *me* what to do?" hissed Queen Malice.

"He's the king!" Trixi darted around and stopped in the air between him and Queen Malice, her tiny arms folded and a very cross look on her face. "You should listen to him!" she yelled.

The queen glared. "Ha! I won't listen to him, and I certainly won't listen to *you*!" She flicked her fingers and a mini thunderbolt flew from them.

Trixi tried to dodge out of the way, but the thunderbolt caught her leaf and she was thrown through the air.

"Trixi!" the girls gasped as her leaf whirled out of control.

Luckily Trixi landed in the heap of sand. She sat on the golden grains and pointed her ring at the queen defiantly, but when she tapped it to try to cast a spell, only a few spluttering sparks appeared. "Oh no," Trixi cried unhappily. "My magic is all gone!"

Queen Malice screeched with laughter. "After today no one in the kingdom will have any magic – I'll have it all!" Her voice rose in triumph. "And it will make me more powerful than ever!"

With a clap of her hands, she vanished – taking all the sand with her!

Ellie, Jasmine and Summer stared in horror. "Now what are we going to do?" exclaimed Jasmine.

With the pile of sand gone, Trixi was left sitting on the cave floor, her leaf beside her. She burst into tears.

"She's right. Without the sand there won't
be any magic for the whole year."

Summer couldn't bear seeing Trixi so
upset. She picked her up gently. "Please
don't worry. There's still time for us to
solve the problem."

"Not much, I'm afraid." King Merry
pointed outside. Night had fallen while
the girls had been in the cave, and Glitter
Beach was bathed in moonlight. "It's
almost midnight."

Trixi started to sob even more loudly.

The girls went to the entrance. Down
on the beach the fairies were fluttering
around like they were lost. The jagged
black edges of the thunderbolt stuck up
out of the rocks, casting shadows as spiky
as Queen Malice's crown.

"There must be a way to fix things,"

said Jasmine, pacing up and down.

"Usually, to break the thunderbolt, we need to reverse the magic," Summer said thoughtfully. "This thunderbolt has stolen the sand. If we can put it back on the beach, then maybe the spell will be broken."

"But we don't have any sand," Ellie pointed out. "Queen Malice has taken it all."

"Not all of it!" Summer gasped. "Look!" She pointed at Trixi. The little pixie's hair and clothes were still coated with fine grains of shimmering sand from when she had been knocked into the pile by Queen Malice.

"But is that enough sand to break the spell?" Ellie said.

"There's only one way to find out!"

cried Jasmine.

With Summer carrying Trixi carefully in her hands, they all ran outside.

Summer had just stepped out of the cave when a bony leg poked out in front of her and she tripped.

"Argh!" she cried, letting go of Trixi as she put her hands out to stop herself from falling.

Trixi managed to catch hold of her leaf and jump on before she crashed to the ground, but as she did so a few of the tiny grains of sand on her clothes fell off. "The sand!" she cried.

An evil laugh came from behind her. A Storm Sprite was flapping towards her, reaching out his bony fingers to grab her.

"Help!" Trixi cried, flying away from him. More and more of the Storm Sprites

were chasing after her now, but Trixi
was too fast for them. As she ducked and
dived out of their reach, more sand fell
from her clothes.

King Merry, Summer, Ellie and Jasmine
stared up in dismay. "What can we do?"
King Merry asked. The girls looked at
one another helplessly.

Ellie tried jumping and catching a
Storm Sprite as he passed overhead, but
he was flying too high. "If only we could
fly!" she said in frustration.

"I know some fairies who can!" Jasmine
shouted, running off toward the beach.

"We have to try and catch some of the
sand," Ellie told Summer. The girls ran
underneath Trixi as she zoomed around
overhead, holding their hands up to catch
the falling grains. King Merry held his
cloak out and tried to catch some too.

"It's impossible!" Ellie cried as more of
the precious sand fell off Trixi's clothes
and was lost in a rock pool below.

Suddenly there was a shout and
Jasmine came running back towards the
cave, looking quite out of breath. Above
her fluttered a cloud of furious fairies.

"Go away, you horrid sprites!" one shouted.

"How dare you steal our sand!"

The fairies flew around the Storm Sprites, keeping just out of reach of their pointy fingers. There were so many fairies that the sprites couldn't see if Trixi was among them. "There she is!" one of the sprites yelled.

"No, she's over here!" another shouted.

The girls looked up. Even they couldn't tell if Trixi was hidden in the whirling mass of fairies!

"Psst!" came a tiny voice from below them. "I'm down here!" Trixi was on the ground, hiding behind a rock.

Jasmine, Summer, Ellie and King Merry crept over to her. The little pixie looked very sad. "I lost all the sand," she cried. "Did you catch any?"

They all checked their hands and clothes, but there was no sand anywhere.

Trixi sighed and her shoulders dropped. She turned to look at the beach. "The sand is supposed to be so beautiful, glinting in the moonlight," she said sadly. "I wish we could have seen it."

"I can!" Summer gasped. She pointed

at King Merry's purple cloak. There,
twinkling like a golden star, was a single
grain of sand!

"Oh, well done, King Merry!" the girls
shouted.

"Hold still, King Merry," Jasmine said,
carefully reaching towards the precious
grain of sand with her nimble fingers.

Summer let out a breath as Jasmine
picked it up. "Quickly! We have to put
it on the beach before the clock strikes
midnight!"

Running as fast as they could, the girls
rushed down to where the sea glinted in
the moonlight.

"Here goes!" cried Jasmine, delicately
placing the glimmering grain onto the
rocky shore.

The girls held hands as the sand

touched the grey rocks. For a second, nothing happened. Then, with a massive crack, the thunderbolt on the beach shattered into black fragments.

Ellie felt something falling on her. It felt like the finest, lightest rain. Looking up, she gasped. "It's raining sand!"

Sand floated down from the sky, shining in the moonlight and tickling the girls' skin. All around the fairies noticed and started to cheer.

"It worked!" cried Trixi as the fairies started to dance and fly, swooping and swirling in the glittering air.

"We did it," gasped Ellie, hugging the others. "We've broken the spell and the sand's back – and just in time!"

King Merry threw his crown into the air in joy. "We've saved the day – I mean, the night – and we've destroyed my sister's last thunderbolt!" He began to dance a jig.

Jasmine grabbed the others' hands and pulled them around in a circle. The sand felt soft beneath their feet and they swirled faster and faster, shrieking in delight. The girls saw Willow and Trixi dancing together nearby in the sky. They waved and the two friends waved back. All around them fairies fluttered excitedly, laughing and shouting for joy.

Trixi swooped down to the girls. "It's nearly midnight!" she cried excitedly. "The midsummer magic is about to start!"

Midsummer Magic

The sand on the beach began to sparkle and glow as if it were made of lots of tiny jewels. The shimmer spread from the beach out into the sea, and even the air seemed to glitter with light. The fairies called out in delight as the glow surrounded them, making them twinkle from their toes to the tips of their wings.

It flooded over King Merry, Trixi, and the girls, too, making their skin tingle and buzz.

"Glitter dust," King Merry said with a sigh of contentment. "The magic is working!"

With a delighted smile he sat down on some nearby rocks.

"Look how happy everyone is," murmured Ellie as two fairies fluttered past, twirling and looping in the air as the clock rang out twelve times.

On the final chime, there was a bright silver flash and then the sparkling sand became a soft shimmering gold again.

"We've all got our magic back for another year, thanks to you," Trixi cried, whizzing up to the girls. "And on Midsummer's Eve, you don't even need

a magic spell or a
pixie ring. Look!"
She pointed in
front of her.
"Shining star!"
she declared.
A star popped
into the air. It
floated towards the
pixie, glittering like a

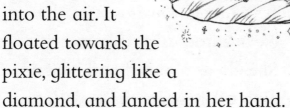

diamond, and landed in her hand.

Ellie remembered what Trixi had said
earlier. "Will we have absorbed any
magic?"

"I don't know," Trixi laughed. "Try
doing some!"

Summer held out her hand rather
cautiously. "Um, a flower!" she said. There
was a bright flash and a gorgeous golden

flower sprang out of the sand! Giggling in delight, Summer bent down and picked it. It smelt amazing!

Ellie couldn't resist. "I'd like a drawing set!" She pointed in front of her and a sketchbook appeared, along with a gold box containing pencils in every possible colour. They floated towards Ellie, the sketchbook opening as if inviting her to draw. She chose a pencil and began to sketch Trixi. When she finished, there was a shimmer and it started to move on the page, waving at her, just like the real pixie. "This is brilliant!" cried Ellie.

"My turn!" said Jasmine excitedly. "I'd love a guitar!" she called, pointing in front of her. Instantly there was a guitar in the air in front of her. Its strings were made of shining gold and it was studded

with bright pink gems. Jasmine whooped
and grabbed it, strumming the strings
happily. She remembered the song she
had once played for the king's birthday
and began to play it now, changing a
few lines:

The Secret Kingdom is a magical place,
Even the moon has a smiley face.
Midsummer's Eve is a time of fun,
Now that Malice's meanness
is quite undone.

As Jasmine's song filled the air, the
fairies joined in and even King Merry
whistled with them. Ellie sang along,
drawing everything that was happening.
Summer made garlands of flowers for
everyone.

When the song ended, King Merry walked over to the water's edge and clapped his hands for silence.

"Once again my sister's wicked plans have been stopped by our three human friends," he proclaimed proudly. "All six thunderbolts have now been found, their magic spells have been broken and the danger to our wonderful Secret Kingdom has passed."

A worrying thought crossed Ellie's mind. It was brilliant that they had stopped Queen Malice, but now that all six thunderbolts had been found, would she, Summer and Jasmine be needed in the Secret Kingdom again? An icy chill ran over her skin. Maybe this was their last visit.

"No," she whispered.

"What is it?" Summer said, seeing her face.

But before Ellie could explain, the king was talking again. "To show my gratitude for all they have done, I have a gift for Summer, Ellie and Jasmine." He patted a silver box on the table next to him. "My dears, would you come up?"

Everyone cheered as the girls walked onto the stage. He handed them a bag made of glittering silver material. On the front of it was a small embroidered crescent – the same shape as the island.

"There is glitter dust in this bag," the king explained as the girls thanked him. "If you need to, you can use it to cast a spell. But use it wisely. There is only enough for one spell each."

Jasmine's fingers tightened on the little pouch as she realised that this gift would fill the final empty compartment in the Magic Box. It was an amazing present, but Jasmine felt like she was about to cry. Did this mean they wouldn't have any more magical adventures? She looked at Summer, whose lip was trembling, and knew she was thinking the same thing.

"King Merry, is this the last time we'll get to visit the Secret Kingdom?" Jasmine burst out.

As the king opened his mouth to reply there was a noise from the sea and a small black boat came flying over the waves.

"It's Queen Malice!" gasped Trixi as the fairies shrieked and cried out.

Two fierce sea serpents pulled the queen's black boat. She stood in the bow, holding long reins and cracking a whip. In the back of her boat crouched the Storm Sprites, jeering and cackling.

Queen Malice pulled the reins and,
with a spray of seawater, the serpents
stopped. "You think you've defeated me,
you pesky brats," she cried. "But I'll be
back! Here's a little something for you to
remember me by!" She clapped her hands
and a thunderbolt shot straight towards
the beach!

"We have to stop it!" Summer cried.
"Can we use magic?"

"Trixi's pixie magic never works against
Queen Malice's spells," Summer said
anxiously.

"But our magic is extra strong tonight
because we've just absorbed so much
glitter dust," Trixi said. "If all the fairies
worked together…"

"And us, we've got magic too!" Ellie
exclaimed.

"It might just work!" Trixi said. She flew high overhead and shouted as loud as she could:

"Fairy friends, this midsummer's night,
Malice's magic we can fight!"

She pointed her hands at the thunderbolt and in an instant every fairy was doing the same. Ellie, Jasmine and Summer copied, and wished as hard as they could that the thunderbolt would break. Suddenly, silvery blue light shot out from their hands.

"It's working!" Summer cried.

The thunderbolt hit the wall of light and shattered into a million pieces, which flew towards Queen Malice.

"Nooooooo!" she screeched, diving

into the water as the shards hit her boat, which broke and started to sink. The Storm Sprites climbed onto one of the sea serpents and helped a soggy Queen Malice onto another. "You haven't seen the last of me!" she shouted as the serpent carried her away. "Just you wait and see!"

Everyone stared after Queen Malice in amazement.

"You asked me whether you will come back," King Merry said softly, as Trixi hovered beside his ear, looking serious. "Well, I have a strong feeling that we will need your help again very soon."

Ellie, Jasmine and Summer looked at one another and smiled.

"We'll come whenever you need us," Jasmine promised. Ellie and Summer nodded.

The fairies all cheered. The air filled with relieved chatter and tinkly fairy laughter.

Jasmine, Ellie and Summer hugged one another. Trixi and the fairies linked hands and flew around them in a glittering circle.

"The Secret Kingdom is safe for now," Summer said, smiling.

"We'll be back again soon," Ellie added.

"And we'll fight whatever Queen Malice throws at us!" Jasmine said.

As they celebrated, Summer's flower garlands faded away. The guitar and sketchbook vanished too, and the girls gave a happy sigh. Their magic had lasted just long enough!

King Merry clapped his hands. "The time has come to say farewell to our human friends – for now." He turned to the girls. "Thank you, from the bottom of all our hearts."

Trixi flew over to them, tears in her blue eyes. "I'll miss all of you so much!" She kissed each of them on the nose. "I've loved the adventures we've had together."

"We'll miss you too," Ellie told her,
feeling her own eyes prickle.

"See you soon!" called Trixi.

Jasmine, Ellie and Summer waved to all their Secret Kingdom friends, then joined hands. Trixi tapped her ring and a sparkly whirlwind started to swirl around the girls.

All around them they could hear fairy voices ringing out to bid them farewell.

"Goodbye!" the girls called as they were scooped up into the air and whisked away.

They landed safely back in Ellie's bedroom. For a moment, they all blinked. "We're home," Ellie said, looking around sadly.

"The box too," said Summer in relief, looking down at the Magic Box, which was now sitting safely on the rug in front of them.

The lid glowed and opened and the

girls placed their precious bag of glitter
dust inside.

"We've had some amazing adventures,"
said Jasmine as the box slowly shut.

"We will go back, won't we?" Summer
asked anxiously.

"Look!" said Ellie as a ripple of light
crossed the mirrored top. They all peered
eagerly into the shining surface. "It's King
Merry and Trixi!" she exclaimed.

The king's kindly face beamed out at
them while Trixi hovered beside him on
her leaf. Words slowly floated up and
formed in the mirror:

Thank you Ellie, Summer and Jasmine.
We will see you again soon!

The girls grinned and waved back in

delight. With a flicker, the image slowly faded and the box returned to normal.

"Yes, we'll go back," Ellie said, feeling certain.

"And we'll see all our friends again," said Summer.

"And have new adventures!" said
Jasmine, her eyes shining.

The three girls smiled at one another.
The Secret Kingdom was waiting for
them. One day the Magic Box would
glow again – and they could hardly wait!

In the next Secret Kingdom
adventure, Ellie, Summer and
Jasmine visit

Christmas Castle

Read on for a sneak peek...

Christmas Eve

"Jingle bells, jingle bells!" Jasmine Smith
sang as she, Summer Hammond and Ellie
Macdonald walked into Ellie's bedroom.

Jasmine twirled round to grin at
her two best friends, her long dark
hair swinging around her. "Oh, I love
Christmas Eve!"

"Me too," said Summer. "And best of all, tomorrow's Christmas Day! What presents do you two want from Santa?"

"A glitter ball for my bedroom," Jasmine said promptly. "And some new CDs."

"I'd really like some new paintbrushes," said Ellie, tucking her red curls behind her ear.

"But you've already got loads!" said Jasmine. Ellie loved art and every inch of her bedroom seemed to be crammed with paintbrushes, paints, pencils and paper.

"You can never have too many paintbrushes," said Ellie. She turned to Summer. "I bet you want something to do with animals."

Summer smiled. "Definitely! I saw a new book about a little lost puppy when

I was at the bookshop last week — I'd love to get that for Christmas." She sighed. "Oh, I hope Santa brings us everything we've asked for."

"We'll have to remember to leave mince pies out for him," said Jasmine. "The ones we've just put in the oven should be ready soon."

"That reminds me," Ellie said, her green eyes twinkling. "What do elves put in their mince pies?"

"What?" said Summer and Jasmine.

"Elf-raising flour, of course!" Ellie laughed.

Summer groaned, and Jasmine threw a cushion at Ellie.

"I wonder what the elves in the Secret Kingdom put in their mince pies," Jasmine said. "I bet they make amazing mince pies at Christmas time!"

The three girls exchanged grins. No one but them knew about the Secret Kingdom, a magical land where all kinds of amazing creatures lived. Summer, Ellie and Jasmine had found out about it by chance when they'd taken home a magical box from their school jumble sale and had been whisked away on an amazing adventure! Since then they'd become the Very Important Friends of King Merry, the ruler of the kingdom, and helped out whenever his horrid sister, Queen Malice, brought trouble to the beautiful land.

"Do you think they have Christmas in the Secret Kingdom?" wondered Summer.

"They must," said Ellie. "It's the most perfect place ever and nowhere could be perfect if it didn't have Christmas! Shall I get the Magic Box?"

"Oh, yes!" said Jasmine.

Ellie rummaged under her bed and pulled out a box about the size of a biscuit tin. Its wooden sides were carved with beautiful pictures of unicorns, mermaids and fairies, and there was a mirror on its lid surrounded by six green gems that twinkled with magic.

Summer touched it longingly. "You know what would be the best Christmas present ever?" she said. "Going to the Secret Kingdom again."

Suddenly a bright golden spark rippled across the mirrored surface of the box. "Look!" Jasmine gasped. "The magic! It's happening again!"

"It's a Christmas miracle!" Ellie laughed.

They all leant forward eagerly as a string of words swirled up to the surface of the mirror. "There's a message for us!" Jasmine said and she read it out:

"Merry Christmas everyone,
Come and have some snowy fun!
Search for a flag and a festive show,
With holly, ivy and mistletoe."

Read

Christmas Castle

to find out what happens next!

Be in on the secret. Collect them all!

Enjoy six sparkling adventures.

Out now!

Secret Kingdom

A magical world of
friendship and fun!

Join best friends
Ellie, Summer and Jasmine at

www.secretkingdombooks.com

and enjoy games, sneak peeks
and lots more!

You'll find great activities, competitions, stories
and games, plus a special newsletter for
Secret Kingdom friends!

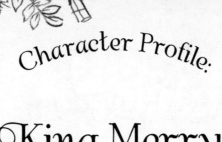

Character Profile.

King Merry

Personality:
Kind and clever
but sometimes
confused. Luckily
Trixi's usually around
to look after him!

Favourite
place in the
Secret Kingdom:
His special
snuggly throne in his
Enchanted Palace.

Guide the Girls

Oh no! The horrid Storm Sprites have trapped
Trixibelle in the Glitter Beach caves! Can you guide
Ellie, Jasmine and Summer and help them find her?

Ellie, Summer
and Jasmine

should take
path

C

A   B   C

I found you trip!

Secret Kingdom Codebreaker

Sssh! Can you keep a secret? Ellie, Summer and Jasmine have written a special message just for you!
They have written one secret word of their special message in each of the six Secret Kingdom books.

To discover the secret word, hold a small mirror to this page and see your word
magically appear!

The first secret word is: _____

When you have cracked the code and found all six secret words,
work out the special message and go online to enter the competition at

www.secretkingdombooks.com

We will put all of the correct entries into a draw and select one winner to receive a special
Secret Kingdom goody bag featuring lots of sparkly gifts, including a glittery t-shirt!

You can also send your entry on a postcard to:

Secret Kingdom Competition, Orchard Books, 338 Euston Road, London, NW1 3BH

Don't forget to include your name and address.

Good luck!

Closing Date: 31st October 2012.

Collect the tokens from each Secret Kingdom book to get special Secret Kingdom gifts!

In every Secret Kingdom book there are three Friendship Tokens that you can exchange for special gifts! Send your friendship tokens in to us as soon as you get them or save them up to get an even more special gift!

3 tokens

5 tokens

7 tokens

13 tokens

15 tokens

Secret Kingdom poster and collectable glittery bookmark

Pencil and rubber set

Pocket mirror

Two best friends friendship bracelets (one for you and one for your best friend)

Glittery t-shirt

To take part in this offer, please send us a letter telling us why you like Secret Kingdom. Don't forget to:
1) Tell us which gift you would like to exchange your tokens for
2) Include the correct number of Friendship Tokens for each gift you are requesting
3) Include your name and address
4) Include the signature of a parent or guardian

Secret Kingdom Friendship Token Offer
Orchard Books Marketing Department
338 Euston Road, London, NW1 3BH

Closing date: 31st October 2012

www.secretkingdombooks.com

1 Friendship Token	1 Friendship Token	1 Friendship Token
www.secretkingdombooks.com	www.secretkingdombooks.com	www.secretkingdombooks.com

Look out for the
next series!

Available
February 2013